Mommy and Me by Ourselves Again

Story and Illustrations by Judith Vigna

Albert Whitman & Company, Niles, Illinois

Other Books by Judith Vigna
Anyhow, I'm Glad I Tried
Couldn't We Have a Turtle Instead?
Daddy's New Baby
Everyone Goes as a Pumpkin
Grandma Without Me
Gregorio Y Sus Puntos
Gregory's Stitches
The Hiding House
The Little Boy Who Loved Dirt and
Almost Became a Superslob
Nobody Wants a Nuclear War
She's Not My Real Mother

Text and illustrations © 1987 by Judith Vigna
Published in 1987 by Albert Whitman & Company, Niles, Illinois
Published simultaneously in Canada by General Publishing, Limited, Toronto
All rights reserved. Printed in the United States of America.
10 9 8 7 6 5 4 3 2 1

Library of Congress Cataloging-in-Publication Data

Vigna, Judith.
   Mommy and me by ourselves again.

   Summary: Unhappy when her mother's former boyfriend
forgets her birthday, a little girl is comforted by
the loving attention of her mother and other relatives.
   [1. Birthdays—Fiction. 2. Promises—Fiction.
3. Mothers and daughters—Fiction. 4. Single-parent
family—Fiction] I. Title.
PZ7.V67Mo 1987   [E]   87-2059
ISBN 0-8075-5232-1 (lib. bdg.)

Mommy's boyfriend doesn't come here anymore.
They had a fight on Sunday and split up.
I miss Gary. Especially today.
It's my birthday.

Last year he came over on my birthday
and gave me a beautiful charm bracelet
with a little blue forget-me-knot charm.
He promised me a new charm on every birthday
for my whole life, so we'd be friends always.

He took me to a real restaurant,
and I had spaghetti and a cake with five candles.
The waiters sang "Happy birthday, dear Amy,"
and everyone looked at me.

Then I made a wish. I wished
that Gary would stay with us forever
and never go away, like Daddy did.
Daddy divorced us when I was little.
He never comes to see me.

My wish didn't come true.
Sometimes I think I made Gary go away.
Once he told me to clean my room and I said,
"I don't have to do what you say.
You're not my real daddy."

But Mommy says it wasn't my fault
that she and Gary split up.
"Gary and I stopped loving each other.
He never stopped loving you."

I don't believe her. If Gary loved me,
he wouldn't have gone away.

I'll never love anyone again, ever.

Sometimes I'm scared that Mommy will leave me, too.
I hate it when she goes away on business trips,
even though I like to stay with Grandpa.

Today Mommy took a vacation day so we could go
to the museum for my birthday treat.

Lots of times it's fun, Mommy and me by ourselves.

We saw a whole family of beavers.
Mommy said they were stuffed,
but I know I saw one move.
There was a father and mother and some babies.
I wished I had a whole family.

We took the elevator to see the dinosaurs.
One was so big it was scary.
But Mommy said there aren't any dinosaurs anymore.
"They disappeared millions of years ago," she explained.

I hoped Gary hadn't disappeared.
I couldn't wait to go home and see if he'd remembered
the charm he promised for my birthday.

But our mailbox was empty. Gary had forgotten!
I felt terrible.
He promised to be my true friend *always*.

I ran into a corner, but Mommy followed me.
She hugged me hard. "I miss Gary, too,"
she said. "And I'm sad that it didn't work out.
But he's gone from our lives now.
It's hard to find someone who's special enough
to be a good husband for me and a good father for you,
but I hope I will someday."

I thought Gary was special.

Just then I heard the bell chime,
and I ran to open the door. It was Grandpa!
With him were Aunt Ruth, Uncle Joe,
and my cousins, Fred and Elise.
"Surprise!" they shouted together.

We all put on funny hats and ate
strawberry ice cream and hot dogs.
My cake was even nicer than last year.
After I opened my big presents,
Grandpa gave me a little box.
"Here's a special birthday present
for you from all of us," he said.

for our
darling Amy
with love

Inside the box on a shiny yellow ribbon
were six charms.
Six little people for my bracelet!
I thought it was because I turned six today.
But Mommy said there was
an even more important reason.

She pointed to the charms and said,
"Pretend these are the six people who love you most—
me, Grandpa, Uncle Joe, Aunt Ruth, Fred, and Elise.
Gary couldn't keep his promise,
but we can keep ours.
We promise that we'll always try to be here for you,
and we'll always love you.

Always."